From the Mouth of the Monster Eel

Other titles in the *World Stories* series:

The Abacus Contest: Stories from Taiwan and China
by Priscilla Wu
Illustrated by Xiao-jun Li

Cloudwalker: Contemporary Native American Stories
by Joel Monture
Illustrated by Carson Waterman

Dog People: Native Dog Stories
by Joseph Bruchac
Illustrated by Murv Jacob

From the Mouth of the Monster Eel

Stories from Micronesia

Bo Flood

Illustrated by Margo Vitarelli

fulcrum kids

Golden, Colorado

For my grandmother
  who sat me on her lap and sang stories to me
For my parents and my children
  who listened to my dreams and didn't laugh
And especially, for Bill

Thank you to the teachers of Saipan, Tinian and Rota who shared their stories and respect for storytelling

Copyright © 1996 Bo Flood
Cover and interior illustrations copyright © 1996 Margo Vitarelli

Jacket and book design by Alyssa Pumphrey

Library of Congress Cataloging-in-Publication Data

Flood, Nancy Bohac.
    From the mouth of the monster eel : stories from Micronesia /
[retold by] Bo Flood ; illustrated by Margo Vitarelli.
        p.   cm.
    Contents: From the mouth of the monster eel — Sirena : cursed from the sea — The tree that bled fish — The monster-lizard of Yap — The first coconut tree — One sail and ten brothers.
    ISBN 1-55591-245-1 (hardcover)
    1. Tales—Micronesia. [1. Folklore—Micronesia.] I. Vitarelli, Margo, ill. II. Title.
PZ8.1.F615Fr   1996
398.2'09965—dc20
                                                96-3449
                                                CIP
                                                    AC

Printed in the United States of America

0 9 8 7 6 5 4 3 2 1

Fulcrum Publishing
350 Indiana Street, Suite 350
Golden, Colorado 80401-5093
(800) 992-2908 • (303) 277-1623

Contents

Introduction

The largest thing in the world is the Pacific Ocean. Its waters span over one-third of the earth's surface. On the many islands and atolls west of Hawaii, stories are told about how all important things came to be.

Imagine it is night and you are sitting on a beach. In the warm darkness, a bonfire flickers light on the face of the storyteller. Smell the salty air. Hear the clatter of coconut fronds above you. Ghost crabs scamper over empty shells near you. Let the sand itch between your bare toes and listen … .

Once upon a time, long ago, there was nothing alive in the ocean. There were no birds or trees, not even any islands. The ocean was empty and lonely. Spirits and people worked and played together to create everything that is. From the islands of Micronesia, far west of Hawaii, legends are told by the oldest and wisest of the storytellers. These legends tell us about how all important things came to be.

From the Mouth of
the Monster Eel

From the Mouth of the Monster Eel

Don't do it!" The counselor warned.

But the king had made up his mind. He governed all the islands and atolls of the Marshalls, hundreds of islands that spread across the Pacific Ocean like stars across the sky.

King Irilik was a powerful ruler. He was also very stubborn, especially when ruling his own children, of which he had dozens. As a parent, he was often too kind and a little foolish. King Irilik loved to escape from his serious duties and sit on the shores of Eebe, the loveliest and most lush of all the islands, and be surrounded by his flocks of children. Flocks indeed, because these children could turn into birds whenever they wished. All day long his daughters and sons played and cavorted, sometimes swimming in the surf but often turning into seabirds, swooping and somersaulting in the clouds.

Like many island fathers, the king was especially fond of his youngest son, Bejwak, a shy and awkward child. He worried about this slow-moving, slow-speaking youngster whose only desire was to play and sing in the surf. Bejwak was teased by his older brothers, especially Jekkar. This brother was dark and quick and often bullied Bejwak. Because of his skill and quick thinking, Jekkar often won first and best. But quiet, slow-moving Bejwak remained first in his father's heart.

King Irilik glared at his counselor, thumped his staff and declared, "Bejwak may seem happy now but I want to ensure his happiness forever. This son of mine needs a special gift, a gift that will protect him through life, the gift of *aao*. Then only good things will come to him."

Aao is the Marshallese name for that special personal charm few people have. A person having aao, which is similar to "halo," has a personality that brings success, friendship and good luck. Unfortunately, Bejwak had very little aao.

The counselor tried one last argument. "Bejwak only seems slow because he is lazy. Everything has been given to him. Bejwak will grow wise by learning from his own efforts and mistakes."

"No, he needs the protection of aao. Go. Find the last remaining lump and anoint my youngest boy. Give Bejwak the gift to guarantee an untroubled life."

"Such a gift is no gift at all."

The king thumped his staff and pointed to the northern horizon.

The counselor wisely left. Shaking his head, he walked away from the village until he found a tall breadfruit tree where he could think under its comforting shade. This task must be completed quickly or his own life would become brief. But what scheme could possibly succeed? The only aao left on earth was hidden somewhere near Jemo, an island far to the north. Getting to such a distant place would be the first of many dangerous problems.

This aao was lodged deep in the throat of the great Mother Eel, the largest of all eels. This monster eel lived far under the ocean's surface in a secret cave. She was the mother of all fish, giant eels and human beings, but she also had a great appetite for eating them. Her black temper was unforgiving and when disturbed, she would snake out from her dark cave, her monstrous body slowly undulating to the surface where she would raise herself high above the waters. Her mouth would bellow out a thunderous roar while her tail would whip the sea into a frenzy of foam and waves. Her beady eyes would search the horizon. Anything alive had little hope of staying that way.

"All for a little aao. Such foolishness," muttered the counselor, but he was beginning to create a plan.

"A giant. I must find a giant, the strongest and boldest one around. It would help if he were a little foolish, too."

In those days there were giants, ghosts and various kinds of monsters. Some were friendly to people and some were enemies. The king's counselor sent for the largest giant alive.

"Amazing. I'd forgotten how tall you fellows stand." The counselor looked up, up, and even higher until he saw a friendly face towering far above the coconut palms. Quickly he ordered, "By the King's own command, go to the island of Jemo. Find the great Mother Eel. Awaken her and take from deep within her throat the last remaining bit of aao." The counselor cleared his own throat and continued. "On your return, I will send Bejwak to meet you. As soon as you see him, anoint him with aao."

The giant nodded. He was eager for adventure. Being one of the largest creatures who walked the earth, he did not know fear.

In those days giants were taller than people now can even imagine. This giant's legs were so long that the ocean only splashed against his knees. His head was lost in the clouds, making it difficult to see where he was walking. And his feet—one misstep and—*squash*—a whole island was sunk.

The first problem for this giant was fitting between the islands and atolls. It was impossible for him to squeeze between most of the volcanic islands without toppling them over. First he waded between the atolls of Jaluit and Ailinglaplap. Unfortunately there wasn't enough space for his bottom to get through. These atolls are only a hundred miles apart.

Then he inched between Ailing-laplap and Namo atolls, but no go. He squeezed between Namo and Kwajalein, but he couldn't get through there either. He thought about jumping over them but was afraid of the splash he might make when landing. And what if he fell down?

At last, he slipped between Kwajalein Atoll and Rongelap where a space of two hundred miles separated them. Then he marched straight north to Jemo where he called on his good friend Bikar and asked for help.

As I have explained, this giant was big. But Bikar was even bigger. He was so tall that he rarely stood up, for when he did, the sun itself was blocked from view across the entire Pacific Ocean. Mostly Bikar sat in the middle of Jemo, making things.

Bikar called back to the giant. "Come sit here by me. First I must finish making this rope." But as Bikar moved his hands to roll the twine away from him, the whoosh of wind made by this movement whipped his friend clear across the ocean. Luckily, Bikar then rolled the twine the opposite way, sucking the giant back to his side. Bikar's laughter tumbled across the sea like thunder. He rolled the rope again, blowing his friend back and forth, back and forth until the rope was finished. The giant was nearly finished too!

"What brings you so far north, my old friend?"

"I have been sent by King Irilik to find the last bit of aao. I must snatch it from whoever guards it and bring it to his youngest son, Bejwak."

"Yours is a sad, sad adventure."

"Why is that?" The giant frowned, still feeling rather dizzy and light-headed.

"The last spot of aao is lodged deep within the mouth of the great Mother Eel."

"Where does she live? I will talk with her."

"Her home is a cave in the deepest, blackest part of the ocean. No one has ever spoken to her and returned."

"But I must explain the purpose of my journey."

"Very well, but remember, she doesn't like to be disturbed." Bikar pointed to the far end of the island's reef. "Her home is somewhere down, down, down beneath the reef's edge." He slowly shook his head. "If I can think of a way, I will help you."

The giant thanked his friend and started walking along the long reef, but hundreds of eels, hidden in the crevices, swarmed out and began biting his toes.

Bikar chuckled when he saw his friend running back toward him. "Already you have the aao?"

"No, no. My feet were being bitten as if I'd stepped into a beehive."

"Sit and rest. I have a plan. Perhaps the two of us can out-trick this monstrous Mother Eel." Without pausing to explain, Bikar grabbed the giant, lifted him up, flipped him upside down and stuck him into the belt of his grass skirt. The giant gasped. He started to yell but quickly closed his mouth. His nose hung only inches above the snapping teeth of the angry eels.

With four colossal leaps, Bikar jumped from one spot to another until he stood at the reef's edge. "Get ready to swim!"

For the first time in his life, the giant felt fear, a paralyzing coldness that gripped his entire body and left him shaking. "S-s-swim? Where?"

"Watch out. Do what I say for here she comes. When her mouth is stretched open, swim between her teeth, reach down into her throat and grab the gooey aao stuck in the folds of her neck."

Before the giant could protest, the sea began to churn around him as if whipped by a monstrous typhoon. White foam tumbled and swirled like spinning mountains. And then the Mother Eel lifted her hideous head, higher and higher.

"Swim! Swim before it's too late!"

But the giant could not make his arms or legs move.

"Swim or we'll be eaten!"

Again the giant tried to reach toward the ugly head but his arms would not obey his thoughts.

Bikar glared at the giant. He grabbed him by the legs and swung him closer and closer to the eel's gaping mouth. Back and forth, closer and closer. The eel opened her mouth wider with each swing. Foul-smelling saliva dripped from her teeth.

Just as the eel was about to snap her mouth over the giant's head, Bikar flung the giant high into the sky. The eel roared a victorious scream. Bikar slipped his hand into the eel's mouth, grabbed the aao, then leaped high to catch his friend before the monster's teeth could snag him.

The poor giant fainted. Bikar caught him with one hand and carried the aao in his other. With one gargantuan jump, he landed safely back in the middle of Jemo, far from the snapping jaws of the monstrous Mother Eel.

Bikar set the giant upright on his feet. "Here is your foolish aao. Go quickly and take it to the King."

The giant, still feeling light-headed and dazed, stumbled back south. Soon he spied a small bird flying toward him. He smiled, remembering the counselor's words: Bejwak, the King's youngest son, would be sent to meet him. This little black bird must be Bejwak.

"Greetings and many thanks, dear giant." The small dark bird landed on the wide shoulder. "What a faithful servant you have been. My father will be pleased."

"Are you Bejwak, the son sent to meet me?" asked the giant.

"Who else could I be?" quickly answered the bird.

"Stand on my finger and bow your head." The giant carefully spread the aao over the bird's head.

Immediately the bird turned into a person. But this person was Jekkar, the older brother of Bejwak. He laughed triumphantly. "I have won the aao from my brother. I am the son most quick and clever."

The crying of another bird was heard in the distance. The giant looked up to see a large brown bird slowly, slowly flying nearer.

The large bird awkwardly landed on the giant's other shoulder. "I have been fooled again by my brother. You have given the aao to Jekkar. But perhaps there is still a little left for me?"

The giant looked at his finger. Jekkar had changed from bird to boy so quickly that a little bit of aao remained. The giant reached over to Bejwak and spread the last remaining aao. There was barely enough to make one thin line across each side of his head.

Now both brothers were anointed with aao, although the quick and clever Jekkar had more. They both had good luck the rest of their lives, but Jekkar was always the luckier. Slow-moving Bejwak remained his father's favorite.

Now when the Marshallese hear the large bejwak birds crying before sunrise, they smile. They know that the day will be good. Bejwak and his children fly from the King's distant shores and merrily sing out the good news. The King is happy and will bless his islands with fish and fruit.

And when the Marshallese sit near the shore watching the little black birds, they laugh. These busy seabirds have heads capped with white as if wearing a halo or cap. Jekkar birds look out only for themselves, flying all day over the waters, their eyes eager for fish, their beaks open for a catch. They fish successfully but sing very little.

Sirena: Cursed from the Sea

Long ago on the island of Guam in the Pacific Ocean, lived a young girl named Sirena. She was always in the ocean, and she was always in trouble. Every day ended with the same scolding from her mother.

"Sirena, again you were swimming, chasing the waves, wasting your time. You must obey the ways of our island. Finish your work and then play. It is the law of our clan, the way we survive."

"But, mother, the sea sings and calls to me."

"My little daughter, listen and obey. The sea swirls with mothers' tears. The ocean is not always our friend."

Sirena nodded. Yes, she would try.

The next morning as the horizon yawned pink with the sunrise, Sirena walked barefoot through cool, long shadows, gathering bananas and breadfruit. Her first chore finished, Sirena sat cross-legged in front of the women's pavilion. She stared at the long strips of pandanus leaves ready for weaving. High above her, slender white tropic birds yapped back and forth scolding one another. They dipped and soared as they sailed on the sea winds.

Sirena began to weave. Her fingers pulled and tugged the long leaves into patterns. She leaned forward, hoping to hear the thundering surf crashing along Agana Bay. As she listened, her heart beat faster and faster but her fingers wove more slowly. Her toes curled and uncurled to the rhythm of the sea's tumbling song. Finally, Sirena stood up and looked toward the bay. The coconut palms above her nodded, *yes, yes.*

Sirena dropped her weaving and hurried down the white coral path to the shore. She smiled as she watched the waves rolling toward her. "Just for a moment—I can play just for a moment."

Over the hot sand she skipped into the water, splashing and scaring pale ghost crabs back into their holes. She hurried from a tall grandfather wave rushing in from the sea. Sirena laughed. After the wave crashed and started slipping away, Sirena chased it back to the ocean. She took a deep breath and *splash!*—into the next wave she dived. She then swam and swam to where the ocean was deep and the water was cool.

Her arms were tired so she floated lazily in the sea. Overhead the clouds made faces at her. Around her the waves lapped. She watched as the waves laced in and out with the sunlight like her weaving. Her weaving!

Sirena raced back to the shore, dashed up the path and quickly sat down next to the unwoven pandanus. Her hair was dripping and her fingers were wet. The leaves slipped this way and that.

She watched her mother slowly walk to the weaving house. Sirena stared down at the puddle of seawater pooling around her. Her mother shook her head and began to scold.

"Such a disobedient daughter! Your weaving is tangled and still unfinished! You have been playing in the ocean, wasting your time, neglecting your work."

Sirena dared not to look up but she spoke out softly. "Mother, why must I weave? Let me go with my brothers and hunt in the lagoon for the lobster and octopus."

"Sirena, you are behaving more like a fish than a child of this island. *Your* work is to sit and weave. As you pull each leaf over and under the others, think, my daughter. If even one leaf slips out of the pattern, the mat will unravel and be useless."

"But mother—"

"It is the same for our people. We must each do our part for all to survive."

Sirena sadly nodded.

"Obey, my child. Stay away from the sea or it will claim you."

Her mother said no more. Sirena looked up, surprised to see tears in her mother's eyes.

"I will try, mother. I will try to do better."

"I must forbid you to swim until you have learned this lesson."

Sirena tried. She would not let her feet follow the path to the shore. She pressed her hands over her ears to shut out the sounds of the sea. But Sirena could not keep out the longings that tugged within her.

Every day Sirena tried to think only about her work. She tended the taro plants, poking her stick near their roots, watching the water swirl with the dirt. She wiggled her toes in the thick mud, remembering how she once laughed when the cold sea sand tickled her bare feet.

Sirena tried to weave the pandanus leaves straight and tight like her Matlina, her godmother, whose fingers seemed to dance with the weaving. Matlina chanted stories as she worked and Sirena listened. But she could also hear the waves crashing on the shore. She imagined she was swimming to catch the next wave and then tumbling over and over as it curled and crashed.

"Open your eyes, silly child. Your weaving is loose and crooked."

"Oh, Matlina, my weaving will never be like yours."

"Because you are thinking of other things."

"I was listening to the surf. Do you hear it, Matlina?"

"Of course, but there is something more I can hear."

"Yes, now I hear it too. Such a sad, sad sound. It seems to echo from the waves. How could that be?"

"I shudder to tell you. We are listening to the weeping of mothers who have lost their children."

Sirena jumped up. "No, no. You are wrong, Matlina. It is only my little brother crying. See him sitting in the sun?" She looked up at her godmother, asking for permission.

"Yes, go to your brother and comfort his troubles. I will straighten your weaving. Bring me back an armful of flowers and we will braid them into a *mwar-mwar* so you will have a crown of blossoms to wear around your head."

Sirena ran to her brother. He was crying and rubbing his feet. "My toes are burning from the sand!"

She swooped him up and carried him to the shade of a breadfruit tree. She rubbed his feet and then broke open a green coconut.

"Hush now and drink the cool coconut milk. When you are quiet, I will tell you a story." Sirena rocked her brother and told him about the needlefish, long and thin as Matlina's fingers. Her hands became the fish moving through the water without making a sound.

"Little brother, these long, see-through fish glide along the top of the water with a hundred of their brothers and sisters. If you swim over to them, they will not dart away. They will only stare at you and they can stare forever, never blinking. Can you?"

Her brother tried, but laughed. Blink! No, he could not stare forever like the fish that swam in Agana Bay.

"Show me these needlefish. We will make faces at them and then they will blink."

Sirena looked past the village, past the coconut trees that leaned toward her as if waiting for her answer. She shook her head. "No, little brother. I cannot. But I will sing about the fish and then I must finish my work."

Her brother jumped up and ran down the path. "Sing to me by the sea. Sing to me there!"

Sirena raced after her brother all the way to the shore. "Now sit still and I will sing. But only one song." She gazed at the ocean and began.

Sirena sang with the beauty of one singing from the heart. Her dark eyes, rimmed with white, sparkled as her words told about the fish swimming fast and free. Her amber skin glowed as warm and smooth as a polished coconut shell. Her hair, black as a starless night, flowed long, long, long, until it curled around her knees. As she chanted, she rocked back and forth, back and forth, and her hair swayed like the swish of palm fronds tossed by the sea wind. But Sirena's smile was sad—the thin, melancholy smile of a new crescent moon.

"Enough, little brother. Now quickly run home. Tell Matlina I will return soon. I will gather for her an armful of flowers."

Sirena wandered along the shore searching for blossoms and fragrant leaves. Both were needed to make a *mwar-mwar*, the woven crown her godmother would braid for her.

From the hibiscus bush, she picked red trumpets. Her nose told her where to find the sweet white plumeria. She plucked yellow blossoms from the rain tree. Soon her arms were heaped full of flowers that reminded her of the flowering coral, blossoms of the sea she had once gathered with her eyes.

She pretended she was not walking, but swimming. She was about to glide around a coral head and peek at shy zebra fish. She spied a silver barracuda streaking past. Sirena smiled, remembering how the anemone would wave their pink fingers and red sponges which grew like flowers on the bottom of the sea.

Sirena sighed. She had weaving to finish and then coconut to scrape. She tossed her head to shake away the thoughts of the sea. When she looked for the path to begin her walk home, she was surprised.

In front of her sparkled Agana Bay. The sharp, salty air tickled her nose. Her eyes blinked from the bright sun on the water. She laughed as she listened to the surf's swoosh and tumble, but then her smile disappeared.

Little fish, washed in by the tide and trapped in pockets of water on the sand, were leaping and dashing in circles, trying to escape. Sirena ran to the rocky shore. She caught the fish and cradled them in the cup of her hand. She stood by the surf and watched for the cycle of waves to bring a grandfather wave. She reached to the tall wave and let the young fish slide free.

The fish darted away with a flick and were gone. Sirena stared at the sea. She shook her head. She had promised not to swim. She thought about the rules of her people and her work waiting to be finished. She did not want to disobey. But the ocean called.

"I will just cool myself for a moment." Indeed she had walked very far in the hot sun. Stones had bruised her feet and branches had scratched her arms. She took one step into the cool water and then another. She did not notice the giant wave that curled above her. The wave crashed down with a roar, rolling her over and over.

She swam to the surface, rubbed the water out of her eyes, and then spit out a mouthful of sand. Sirena laughed and laughed. She dived into the next wave and then the next. She sang with the clinking of the tumbling shells as she swam through the surf.

She ducked under the waves as they crashed and toppled. Until she remembered. *No swimming. No swimming until the taro was tended, mats were woven and cream was squeezed from the coconut meat.* Her mother's warning had been clear. No swimming, or this time her punishment would be severe.

Sirena caught a wave and raced back to shore. She ran home to finish her work. But in front of the weaving hut, her mother stood waiting, trembling with anger.

"My lazy daughter, again you have disobeyed. When the village learns of your foolishness, they will send you away unless I punish you first. Sirena, you are forbidden to swim. Forbidden! Not ever again!"

"No, mother, no! I cannot stay away from the ocean. Not forever."

"You must or your disobedience will be cursed. You will be claimed by the sea and become nothing but an ugly fish. Your skin will thicken into scales, your hair will tangle into foam and your feet will twist into fins!"

Matlina heard the mother shouting. She knew that angry words from a mother's heart, if heard by the spirits, can turn into a lasting curse. Matlina turned to Sirena. She loved the little girl, even when she disobeyed.

The godmother called, "Listen and obey. To disobey your mother is to disobey your people. When you were newly born I christened you to protect your spirit. But I cannot protect you from your mother's words. You must obey and *never* swim in the sea again."

Sirena shook her head. She could not believe the terrible words. *No,* her spirit cried, *no!* Sirena turned and ran.

Down the path she raced. She heard her mother running to catch her, calling to her to come back.

Sirena shook her head and ran faster. Now she could see the ocean, the sunlight sparkling on the waves. Her legs were trembling. Her heart was beating so fast, so loud, like a chant drumming in her head. Her mother was closer now and crying, "Sirena, come back."

But Sirena ran and ran until she stood on the cliff above the sea. She paused when she heard Matlina's plea.

"Stop, Sirena! Please, you must stop. Do not go in that ocean. Nothing can undo a mother's curse. Nothing."

Sirena was afraid but she did not hesitate.

She leaped into the water, shuddering at the thought of never again having legs—never having arms to hold her little brother while comforting his troubles.

As she leaped she heard Matlina call out to the heavens. "Spirits of the wind and sea, you cannot undo a mother's words, but soften them, soften them. Let the heart and spirit of Sirena be saved."

Sirena plunged into the ocean. The air was torn from her chest. Pain shot through her heart as her body twisted with change. Her legs fused into a powerful tail fin. Her skin thickened into iridescent scales shimmering with the colors of the rainbow. But her upper body, her heart and mind, remained unchanged, the singing spirit of Sirena.

Even today, if you swim in the wrinkled waters of the Pacific, you will see the needlefish, long and thin as a grandmother's fingers, their black eyes unblinking. Shy zebra fish still dart between the cauliflower heads of coral. If you are lucky, you may also see Sirena, half fish and half girl.

Some Chamorros of Guam say that if you watch the waves sweep over the blue, you might see her swimming as swiftly as a barracuda or leaping and playing in the foam. If you stand by the rocks where you can hear the clinking-tinkling of the shells, there in the tumbling rhythm of the surf, Sirena sings:

Go where the water is cool and clear.
Listen to the ocean, listen to your heart.
You will feel my spirit and then you will hear your own.

The Tree That Bled Fish

Kodep licked his fingers, smacked his lips and rubbed his full, full stomach. He leaned back in the warm, soft sand and gazed up at the strange tree that had fed him his favorite food, fish. Long branches spread above him like a wide, green umbrella. Leaves as large as a giant's hands shaded him from the hot sun. Kodep was tired but satisfied. He would not need to chop off another branch until evening.

His cutting stone lay heavy and smooth in his hand. He fingered the sharp edge. He would sleep first and then finish his work. One slash of a limb and the tree would bleed seawater filled with fish. He could quickly catch all he needed for the village. Yes, there was time to rest.

As he closed his eyes and began to doze, a sad moaning drifted into his dream. Cries from an old woman seemed to twist in and out between wakefulness and sleep. Kodep sat up. He rubbed his eyes and glanced around. Nothing. He peered above. The green ceiling of leaves rustled with angry chatter and frowned down at him like flat, angry faces.

"Indigestion!" Kodep glared back. "Too much fish in my big belly." He rubbed his stomach and then wiggled into a more comfortable position. Once again he glanced around. Nothing. He closed his eyes and started to yawn but before he even had his mouth open, a sad moaning called his name.

"Kodep! Remember the warning, Kodep."

"Whoever you are, go away! Go away!" Kodep looked in every direction. He stared so hard that the jungle bushes and vines blurred into a wall of green. He could see no one. All around him was the hush-hush quiet of a jungle when all the little creatures are frightened and waiting.

"Whoever you are, tell me why you are trying to scare me." There was no answer. "Are you the old woman who gave us this tree? If you are, then why are you calling?"

Kodep remembered the story his father had told him about this strange tree that bled fish. Long ago, when the whole village was starving, this tall giant tree appeared. Some people thought they heard words whispered by an ancient spirit. Some people said the whispers were only the wind whipping through the palm fronds. The message, if there had been a message at all, was simple. "Be mindful of this tree. Care for it and it will care for you. Take too much and there will be nothing."

At first the villagers were afraid to venture near the tree. But one day when a branch was broken off, water filled with fish streamed out. Eventually, people came to the tree, rather than the lagoon, to catch fish. Now, every day it was Kodep's job to cut off a branch and catch the fish that poured forth.

Kodep gripped his cutting stone and shrugged. "If I cannot rest then I will work." He scrambled up the tree and began chopping. "Augh!" The branch beneath his feet snapped and he crashed to the ground, landing, splat, in a puddle of seawater, fish and mud.

Once again, a sad whispering hissed through the trees. An old voice scolded. "Do not cut another limb. This tree was given to all so children could survive drought and typhoon. Let the tree blossom and its fruit will feed you."

Kodep stared at the thick jungle grass surrounding him. Tall, thin shadows leaped and danced as if to tease and mock. But he could see no one in the shadows, no one hiding, only grass and shadows whipped back and forth by the wind.

He grabbed his basket and ran pell-mell back to the village. People watched as he raced toward them, bumping his basket in front of him.

Kodep looked at the staring faces and told about the sad voice.

The little children giggled. No one in the village had heard any whispers or moans. Older boys pointed and laughed. "Kodep, you are trying to trick us. You ate too many fish before you fell asleep and now you are afraid of your own bad dreams."

The old women and men did not laugh. They looked at the lagoon where no one had fished for months. They looked at the villagers making fun of Kodep. They walked silently to their huts.

People ate their evening meal in silence, looking at one another as if to ask, *Did you hear the sad voice crying? Of course it was only the whoosh and whispers of the wind!* People returned quickly to their huts, unrolled their mats and tried to sleep.

The next day Kodep asked his friends, "Help me gather fish. Today we will cut many branches and fill every basket. Tonight we will heap wood onto a leaping fire, eat until we are bursting and dance until we sleep."

They followed him and then gathered around the tree's tall trunk. Kodep hesitated, listened, but heard nothing. He threw back his head, laughed, and then quickly climbed to the tallest limb. He gripped his cutting stone and pierced the gray bark. Seawater trickled out. A gust of wind slapped through the giant leaves and a soft moan seemed to cry from the tree.

"Foolishness! A tree is nothing, only a tree! Meant to be cut, to bleed, to die," Kodep thought. He sliced again, deeply, swiftly.

A scream pierced the silence. There was no doubt. An old woman's voice pleaded. "Do not harm this tree, this breadfruit tree, given to all generations. Do not kill it arm by arm. Protect its life and this tree will nourish you with bread."

Kodep's friends argued that the voice was the trick of some evil spirit. "Cut the tree down once and for all and never return to this bewitched place. Hack it down. Destroy the evil spirits before they destroy us."

Kodep stared at the seawater seeping from the wound. If he didn't bring back fish, the people would mock him and throw rocks. He gripped the cutting stone and raised his arm.

The echo of the scream would not leave his head. "Someone is calling me. I don't understand but I must find who it is." He began walking away from the village and toward the source of the cries.

He walked until he came to the far end of the island where only a few coconut palms and deserted taro patches grew in a tangle of thick, dark jungle. The voice led him to a hut tucked far under the jagged rocks of a lava cliff. Inside the hut an old woman waited. She spoke before Kodep could see into the hut's darkness.

"I cry for the tree. This tree will nourish you with its fruit," she said. "It is the only tree of its kind and you are destroying it branch by branch. If it dies you will have nothing. If it lives, it will provide food."

Kodep was confused. "But the tree gives us fish. I am satisfied with fish."

"Because you do not think beyond today. Fish swarm in the lagoon. Hunt wisely, letting the fish replenish themselves, and you will always have fish." The old woman pointed toward his village. "Care for this tree. Do not kill it. Act wisely and you will always have fruit, the breadfruit."

"If I return without food, the people will be angry and throw stones."

The woman said nothing.

"If I tell them your words, they will laugh and call me a fool. Why should they hunt fish in the lagoon when fish bleed from this tree? They will never believe your words."

The woman said nothing.

Kodep thought about the breadfruit tree he had often climbed. Many branches remained, but many more were gone.

Kodep returned to the village. The people gathered around him, asking many questions.

"Where were you, Kodep, napping again? But where is our supper? Where are the baskets of fish? Our stomachs are rumbling."

Kodep repeated the old woman's words. "It is time to hunt in the lagoon and let the tree rest and its fruit ripen."

The people laughed. "You have been dreaming. This tree has never grown fruit. You are just lazy, making excuses so you won't have to work."

Kodep again explained the old woman's message.

"Kodep, your job is to gather fish from the tree. Go!" Several young men stooped down to pick up rocks.

The chief stepped forward. "We will wait one year. The tree will rest and we will watch for this fruit called breadfruit. After a year, if there is no breadfruit, we will begin chopping."

Many months passed before blossoms appeared in the highest limbs, hidden between pairs of leaves. More months crept by before bumpy green fruit was seen hanging from thin stalks. The people whispered and pointed to Kodep.

Slowly the fruit grew and grew, becoming round and heavy. Kodep once again climbed up the tree with his cutting stone. He raised his arm but this time he cut off large green fruit, breadfruit.

Breadfruit was placed in the evening fire and roasted with the reef fish on top of steaming banana leaves. After the fire burned down to ashes, the breadfruit was given to the chief to taste. He looked at Kodep and nodded. Kodep picked up a blackened fruit, peeled off the outer skin and poked a piece of the hot yellow fruit into his mouth. The villagers and the chief watched. Kodep began chewing.

Kodep smiled. He ate another piece and then another. He rubbed his stomach. First the chief, then the elders and finally the children began nibbling the chunks of roasted breadfruit. Soon everyone was eating until one by one they sighed, licked their fingers, smacked their lips and rubbed their full, full stomachs.

Ever since that evening, even during times of famine, drought or typhoon, breadfuit trees on the islands of the Pacific are honored and protected. Roasted breadfruit often fills hungry stomachs. Children lick their fingers, smack their lips and whisper, "Thank you, breadfruit tree."

The Monster-Lizard of Yap

Long ago on the island of Yap there lived a lizard. Not an ordinary catch-me-if-you-can sort of lizard but a greedy sea monster with an enormous appetite. Whoever dared to sail or swim across the lagoon's surface, the lizard ate.

This lizard's name was Galuf. Some say he had the mouth of a giant crocodile. Indeed, Galuf's jaws were so long, so big and so lined with rows and rows of needle-sharp teeth that Galuf could slip his jaws around an entire outrigger canoe. With one crunch, Galuf would eat the canoe, paddles, people and all.

Needless to say, few dared to visit Yap. Even fewer tried to sail away for help. In time, Yap became a lonely island.

At that time Yap was one large island, not a cluster of islands with sea canals flowing gently in between. Because of this giant lizard's greed, this one island became four: Rumung, Map, Fanif and Mil. But when Yap was still one, the monster Galuf lived in the middle of the area of Mop called Mil. From the middle of Mil, Galuf kept one eye or the other wide open, searching for signs of anyone venturing across the lagoon. But what Galuf did not know was that as he was watching, he also was being watched.

The young man, Pirow, barely old enough to be considered a warrior, had sworn to the spirits of the sea that he would somehow free his island and his people from the monstrous appetite of Galuf.

Pirow watched as Galuf snaked through the lagoon waters. He clenched his fists remembering all the lost warriors who had tried to slay this lizard. Pirow wanted to empty this monster's belly forever. He wanted the waters around Yap to welcome navigators, travelers, and fishermen. As he watched, Pirow began to create a plan.

He saw how the lizard could dart like a javelin from one rocky shore to another. *Speed,* Pirow thought. To defeat this monster he would need to build a canoe, so sleek and so fast that he could out-paddle Galuf. He needed a canoe that could sail faster than the lizard could swim. But how would he know if he was successful? How fast was fast enough?

Pirow explained this puzzle to his wife. She knew there was little chance that her young husband could build such a vessel. If Pirow was not to become Galuf's next meal, the wife suggested that Pirow's canoe must sail faster than a fish could be cooked.

First Pirow went to the forest. He chose a tall sturdy ironwood tree. He gave thanks to the tree spirit, felled the tree, hollowed it out, shaped it properly and dragged it to the water's edge. From this hidden cove, far from the area of Mil, Pirow signaled to his wife. She placed a fish on her cooking fire. Pirow paddled furiously across the cove. He jumped out of the outrigger and raced to his wife who pointed to the burnt fish. The ironwood canoe was too heavy and too slow.

Pirow again searched through the forest. He came to a small clearing at the top of a knoll and spotted a towering coconut palm. Again he gave thanks to the tree spirit, picked up his axe and began chopping. After many days of scraping, Pirow carried out of the forest a sleek, light outrigger to the cove. He signaled to his wife. She signaled back, and then Pirow sprang into the canoe, let out the sail and paddled faster than ever. When he arrived at his wife's side, she sighed and pointed to the charred ashes of the second fish.

This time when Pirow wandered through the forest, he thought about which tree grew slowly so the wood was dense and could be scraped thin but remain strong. He looked at many trees and searched for one which grew tall and straight so the outrigger would slice through the water faster than a spear pierces the air.

Pirow became weary. He rested where the shade was dark. He looked up and smiled back at the enormous leaves above him. The leaves were larger than his head and deeply edged as if circled with laughing smiles.

"The breadfruit tree! Of course. This tree grows slowly but with pride. It has the courage to stand tall yet give generously of its fruit." Pirow closed his eyes and prayed silently to his ancestors and to the spirits. Did he have their permission to cut down such a mighty tree?

The forest grew still. The little geckoes hid and quieted their chirping. Overhead the slender, white tropic birds landed, watching in silent pairs along the tallest limbs. Even the dancing of butterflies seem hushed. The forest creatures waited for Pirow's decision.

And then for many days the only sound was the chop-chop-chopping of Pirow's axe.

Pirow asked his wife to help him carry this slender canoe to the cove. She then ran back to their hut, stirred dry wood into the red coals until they blazed into searing flames. She waited until Pirow raised his hand and gave the signal. Quickly she placed a fish in the hottest part of the fire.

Pirow paddled across the cove, raced back to the hut and stood in front of his wife. This time she pointed to a fish that was still flopping in the fire.

Pirow was pleased. But still he sat frowning, feeling discouraged. He pondered about one last problem. He was quite sure he could sail faster and out-distance the lizard. But how could he kill the monster? Speed alone was useless. *Escaping* the monster accomplished nothing. He must destroy Galuf so others could sail safely across the lagoon.

And then Pirow smiled. He returned to the cove, swam to the deepest part and began diving. He searched and searched until he caught what he needed—a giant clam. When its two shells stretched open, scarlet edges encircled a gaping cavern wider than a shark's mouth.

With the clam tied securely on his outrigger, Pirow entered the lagoon. He began paddling across the widest part.

Soon the monster-lizard also slipped into the water. He slapped the sea with his tail, sending waves spilling in every direction. With a roar of a thousand waterfalls, Galuf challenged his opponent and then dove, swimming full speed toward the slender craft.

But the race was futile. Pirow let out his sail, caught the wind fully and paddled across the waters twice as fast as the monster could swim. Back and forth, all day long the two raced. Finally even the sun tired of this useless chase and slipped beneath the horizon. Now the stars twinkled in amusement.

Again Galuf slapped his tail. He opened his jaws but this time his roar was a tired, whiny voice. "I'm worn out and hungry," he complained. "Let us both rest until morning."

Pirow agreed.

Galuf eyed the slender boat. His stomach rumbled with emptiness. The lizard slowly slithered toward the canoe. To Galuf's surprise, Pirow did not even try to escape. Instead Pirow invited the monster to rest his head on the outrigger.

Once on the boat, the first sight that caught Galuf's attention was the gaping mouth of the clam. How tender and sweet the center would taste. Faster than the skip of a flying fish, the greedy lizard stuck his head into the shell. The clam snapped shut, trapping Galuf's head inside.

The monster roared! But his head was stuck tight and wouldn't budge. He swung his huge tail from side to side, wrestling to break free. With a monstrous heave he slapped his tail down the middle of the island, breaking off the two pieces of Rumung and Map.

Still Galuf struggled to escape. The lagoon waters churned and froth filled the air as if from the winds of a typhoon. Once again the monster-lizard roared, raised his tail and, *whack!*—the hills of Gagil were struck, causing a quaking of the earth and a splitting of the ground. Again the land was separated. No longer was Yap one island, but four—with sea channels the size of Galuf's tail flowing in between.

One last time Galuf swung his tail high. It landed with a mighty splash spilling water everywhere and washing the giant clam, with the lizard's head stuck tightly inside, down to the black bottom of the sea.

These events happened centuries ago. Generations of children have grown up and become grandparents since the islands of Yap were separated by Galuf's tail. Whenever travelers return to their families and navigators arrive from afar, people remember: How good to be together! Food is gathered and singing and dancing begin.

While evening fires flicker and children with empty stomachs are waiting, mothers gather their little ones near. They point to the fish frying in the hottest coals and begin an ancient story. "Once there was a young boy named Pirow who had cunning and courage—and a very wise wife. Listen, and you'll hear how one day Pirow outwitted Galuf, the monster-lizard of Yap."

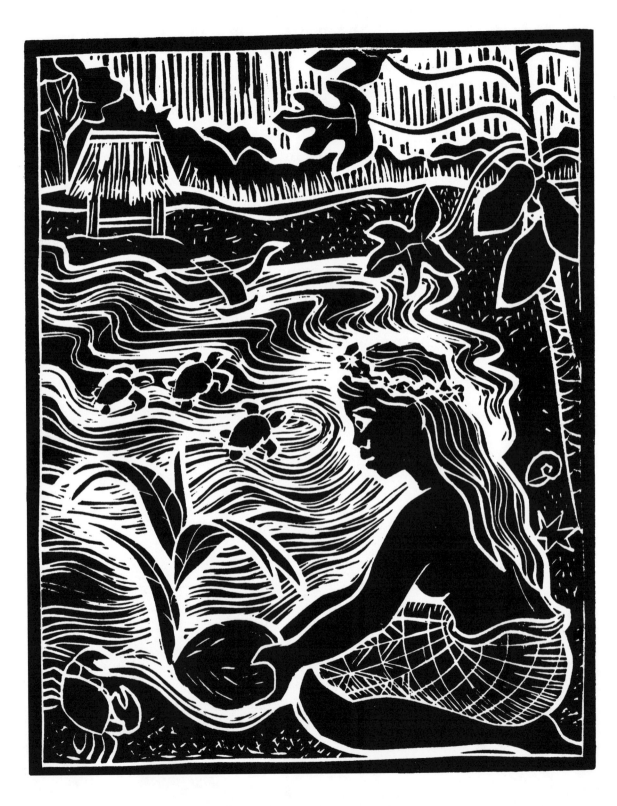

The First Coconut Tree

Long ago on the islands in the Pacific Ocean, there were no trees. No one could even imagine what a tree might be. One day, on the tiny atoll of Ailing-laplap, a baby was born. This child, Debolar, was so round and so ugly that his older brother wanted to kill him. No one suspected that Debolar would bring something that would change all the islands for-ever. Debolar would bring the first tree, the most important tree, though not as you might expect. This is his story.

When Debolar was born, people came from every vil-lage on atoll Ailing-laplap to see this strange baby. Debolar was round and green. He was mostly a face on a very round tummy. He had no arms or legs.

Debolar's older brother was embarrassed. "Kill it! Kill it," he shouted to their mother, Limokare.

Limokare was unsure and asked the other women. "Who can explain why this strange child was born to me, malformed, and so ugly? Perhaps it is a spirit-child that will bring harm to all of us."

As the baby stared up at her, Limokare gazed back at the bright eyes. She saw that they were full of cleverness and caring. She reached down to hold her baby. "I cannot kill you. Sometimes when someone comes into the world unexpected and not understood, they are laughed at instead of valued. No, I cannot kill you. Grow, little round one, and let us see what is within you."

As person after person stared at the ugly baby, the older brother became even more embarrassed. He was ashamed. Again he pleaded, "Before this thing brings evil, kill it. Quickly! Act wisely and kill it."

But Limokare already loved her funny-faced child. She cared for him as tenderly as she cared for his older brother. It seemed this baby, young Debolar, needed a lot of caring. He was always hungry. He drank and drank the sweet milk from his mother. He grew and grew. But he grew only rounder and browner, always with his middle full of milk.

One day Debolar said to his mother, "Bury me in the sand."

"Bury you? But you will die!"

"No, no, mother, I will not die. Bury me in a shady place and each day bring clear water for me to drink."

"Bury you alive? How can I do such a thing?"

"So I can live. I have been nourished by your milk and love. Now I must eat and drink of the earth and be warmed by the sun. I will grow and reach toward the clouds until my fingers can dance in the wind. Then every part of me will be useful. From me, our people will have satisfying food, roofs for their huts, strong rope for building boats and soft mats on which to sleep. My middle will always hold milk for the little children."

Limokare did not understand. She could not imagine what her son would become. How could he survive buried in sand?

Debolar described how he would grow, stretching toward the sky, unfolding his leaves. After many months, he would stop growing and blossoms would appear between his arms. These blossoms would become new babies.

Again he instructed his mother. "Care for these funny round children. Bury them in soft sand. Soon there will be dozens and then hundreds of my children and grandchildren. They will make their way to other villages. The ocean currents will carry them to faraway islands."

Limokare shook her head but did as her son asked. She buried Debolar in the sand just outside the window of her hut. Every evening she brought him fresh spring water. Every day she looked for some change, some sign of life, but sadly she saw none.

One evening, when she was pouring a gourd of water, she saw a small, green sprout. She looked more closely. A thin, curled-up sprout had pushed through the sand. She opened the slender green leaf that was folded around itself like the wet wings of a flying fish. "How beautiful. But what are you? Could you really be my child, my Debolar?"

Limokare gave the folded leaf a name, *drir-jojo,* words meaning sprout *(drir)* and flying fish *(jojo).* Each evening she brought more water. The green shoot grew rapidly, changing size and appearance, and always growing tall toward the clouds. For each change, Limokare called Debolar a new name. Many of these names, *ni, niyog, niu, and drir-jojo,* are still used today.

Many months passed. Debolar grew into a towering tree. His trunk was strong yet supple like the sturdy legs of island children. He sprouted green branches or fronds that reached in all directions. His arms were sometimes quiet but often they were wild and noisy, swaying and laughing in the sea winds, dancing and chattering to his mother who sat beneath in his cool shade.

Limokare remembered what Debolar had once said. She told his words to the other villagers. "Every part of this coconut palm is useful to us. New fruit will continue to grow. Some we will plant and some we will eat. Some will float many miles to other islands. The long fingers of the fronds are strong and can be woven into mats, sails and even roofs. The oil in its meat can flavor our food and protect our skin. Honor this tree, this thing that began as an ugly round baby. Take care of him and he will serve us always."

If you laugh and think it is impossible for a baby coconut to drink milk, just look inside. A fresh young coconut is filled with milk, just like Debolar. Coconut milk refreshes and nourishes, especially the little babies who live on the Pacific islands. If you break open a young coconut, its sweet meat can be eaten like pudding. With time, the meat inside dries and hardens and can be scraped out and washed. The coconut oil or cream is squeezed out and cooked with fish or vegetables.

The coconut tree or *ni* was once essential to the survival of life on the Pacific islands. Other island cultures have their own legends about how this important tree came to be. The coconut palm provides food that can be stored and saved. Every part is used—the leaves, wood, bark, roots, nuts, husks and juices. Rope made from husk fibers is strong and durable. During typhoons, island people once lashed themselves to the trunks of coconut palms. These tough trees can bend in half from hurricane winds and not be blown away.

One Sail and Ten Brothers

Timur, Lomij-drikdrik, Labwal, Ar, Majlep, Dra-im-kobban, Titata, Lok, Jabe, Jabro! The ten brothers of Woja each wanted to be chief, or *Iroij,* of the island Jeh. They argued. They fought. Finally they decided to have a race. They would paddle outrigger canoes across the lagoon from the atoll Woja to the island of Jeh. The winner would be crowned *Iroij!*

Liktanur was the mother of these ten boys. She was one of the brightest stars in the night sky. Often she visited her earth children, sometimes to praise them but usually to scold. She was a wise parent and always watchful.

The race was officially declared. Each brother began building an outrigger canoe and carving strong paddles. Liktanur observed each son's way of working. She shook her head, listening as the bigger boys boasted of their skills and teased the younger ones with insults. The oldest son,

Timur, claimed he could paddle faster than the speed of a striking eel. The middle son puffed up his chest and proclaimed he could paddle farther than any seagull could fly.

Each son claimed a special type of strength except the youngest and smallest, Jabro. He said nothing. Sweat dripped off his back as he worked on his tiny boat, scraping out the tree trunk with shells, rubbing the outside with sand and then oiling and polishing until his canoe was as smooth as a mango skin.

Liktanur looked from oldest child to youngest. She smiled, watching. Which son would have the courage to grant her the unusual request she would make in the morning?

When dawn swept away the last of the night's sky, Liktanur appeared on the beach. In each arm she carried a heavy bundle. She waited as her sons pulled their outriggers to the water's edge, arranging themselves by age. Liktanur approached the oldest boy, Timur, as he raised his arm to signal the race's start.

"My brothers, begin! The winner shall be crowned chief forever!" Timur heaved his canoe into the water, glanced up, and was surprised to see Liktanur standing by his boat. "Mother, why are you here?"

"Let me ride with you."

Timur eyed her heavy bundles, thinking how the weight would slow his boat. "This race is too dangerous." He shook his head. "I shall be crossing the open sea and look, the clouds are piling high and dark. The wind is blowing strong from the east."

"I am not afraid. The sea is home to me. It is no deeper than the sky."

Timur saw that two brothers were already climbing into their canoes. "My craft is too small. Ride with another!" He pushed his boat farther from shore and leaped aboard. Without looking back, he paddled away.

Liktanur walked over to her next oldest son, Lomij-drikdrik. He too was wading deeper into the water, pushing out his outrigger. He frowned when he saw his mother approach, carrying her heavy load. He didn't wait for her to speak but shook his head, waved good-bye and paddled away.

Liktanur walked along the beach and made the same request of each son. One after another, each son refused.

"My boat is too narrow," explained Labwal.

"Too slow," mumbled Ar.

"Much too tippy," said Majlep, and so on until there was only one son left—Jabro, the youngest. Liktanur watched as he struggled to drag his outrigger to the shore. With one last heave, Jabro freed his boat from the beach. The outrigger tipped with the first wave, spilling Jabro headfirst into the water. Another wave swelled and rolled under the boat, pushing Jabro back into the choppy sea. He bobbed back up, sputtered out seawater and then tried again. Soon Jabro and his mother were both laughing at his struggles.

Liktanur waded into the waves and took tight hold of the boat. When Jabro had climbed aboard she asked, "Let me ride with you."

Jabro raised his eyebrows. "You want to ride in my small boat?"

She nodded.

"Mother, we may sink," he pointed to her heavy load, "but at least we will sink quickly." Jabro laughed. "Hand me your things and come aboard."

"Wait. I must unpack before you race."

"But we need to hurry. Look. The others are already out of sight."

Liktanur slowly untied her bundles. Piece by piece she took out two poles, coconut twine and a huge triangular canvas woven from pandanus leaves. "Do not worry about winning. Courage and loyalty, not power, are needed for a child to become chief. Feel the wind. Soon we will fly past the others."

Jabro did as his mother instructed.

"Raise up this pole. I have woven this sail to use with this mast, the *kiju*. Tied together, the mast and the sail will obey your commands. This sail will capture the wind and give you wings on the sea."

Again, Jabro followed his mother's unusual requests.

Liktanur arranged the canvas, twine and poles until the rigging was complete. "Position the *repakak* and the *jirukli* at each end of your outrigger. With these you can alter the boom and always command the wind."

Jabro hoisted the sail. The pandanus rippled with life as it filled with wind. Off raced the boat, flying like a gull skimming over the sea. Liktanur showed Jabro how to keep a steady course by tacking with the *repakak* and *jirukli.* One by one they passed each of his brothers, except for Timur.

Liktanur smiled. "Jabro, you shall be remembered as *Iroij* of Jeh, Liktanur's loyal son who was given the first sail, catcher of the wind."

Finally Jabro caught up with Timur. For a long time the brothers raced evenly, Jabro carefully tacking and Timur paddling furiously. But then Jabro sailed steadily ahead.

Timur shook his fist, yelling, "Give me your boat!"

Jabro looked at his mother, "What can I do? My older brother must be obeyed."

"Give him your boat, the mast and sail." Liktanur smiled. "But unless Timur asks, don't give the *repakak* and the *jirukli.*"

Jabro understood his mother's scheme.

Timur climbed into Jabro's canoe, demanding the sail and the mast. Jabro and his mother boarded Timur's boat and paddled straight for the island.

Howling in triumph, Timur hoisted the sail and away he flew—in the wrong direction. He did not know how to turn the sail and tack toward Jeh. In disgust, he finally ripped the sail down, picked up his paddle and raced toward Jeh, but too late to catch his youngest brother.

Jabro arrived first. Liktanur immediately commanded, "Go to the other side of the island. The villagers will prepare you for tonight's celebration. You will be crowned with a new name—Jabro-Jeleilon, *Iroij,* the Wind-Catcher."

One by one each brother landed on Jeh not knowing who arrived first. They began to quarrel. The evening star appeared and climbed higher to get away from the angry grumbling.

Liktanur ordered her squabbling sons to gather around her. She commanded them to hush and then began to chant:

"Iroij Jabro-Jeleilon—oo!
Jeleilon is king!"

Jabro-Jeleilon stepped forward, his dark skin gleaming with scented oils. He walked slowly and proudly, wearing a royal crown of sacred leaves.

"Iroij Jabro-Jeleilon—oo!
Jeleilon is king!"

The villagers cheered. The brothers ceased arguing and joined in the celebration chant. Except Timur. Frowning and grumbling, Timur turned away, alone, glaring toward the setting sun.

As each brother completed his life on earth, Liktanur brought her sons up to the night heavens. To this day, if you search the night sky over Woja, Jeh or any of the Marshall Islands, the ten brothers shine brightly, each in his correct position to guide ocean voyagers. Timur faces west; Jabro faces east. These two stars still never look at each other. The only star close to Jabro is the mother star, Liktanur.

When children of the Marshalls prepare to become voyagers, they are taught the ancient seafaring secrets. The ten navigational stars are learned through chants that tell of their names, positions and stories. Looking up at the dark Pacific sky, one can find the ten brothers and see the most famous star of all—Jabro, *Iroij:* catcher-of-the-wind, bringer-of-the-sail.

From west to east:

Timur, Lomij-drikdrik, Labwal, Ar, Majlep, Dra-im-kobban, Titata, Lok, Jabe, Jabro!

Glossary

ANEMONE: An invertebrate sea animal, often brightly colored, that looks like a blooming flower.

ATOLL: A circular, often doughnut-shaped coral island surrounding a lagoon that has a "middle" of seawater.

BREADFRUIT TREE: A tall tropical tree used by Pacific islanders for many purposes. Its football-shaped fruit is baked and eaten, tasting something like bread.

CHAMORROS: The island people native to Guam and the Northern Marianas Islands, who are part of the cultural group called Micronesians and are related to the Polynesians.

GHOST CRAB: A small shore crab whose thin shell gives off a pale and ghostly appearance.

LAGOON: A shallow part of the ocean near land that is partially or completely enclosed by coral reefs or atolls.

MANGO: A tropical fruit that is oblong, orange or green-skinned and tastes like a ripe peach.

MWAR-MWAR: A wreath woven from flowers and vines that is worn like a crown as a symbol of celebration.

OUTRIGGER CANOE: A native Pacific wooden canoe with special supports (outriggers) extending out from the side to increase stability.

PALM FRONDS: The leaves of the palm tree, long in shape and particularly light so they clatter with the slightest breeze, but strong and tough enough to withstand typhoon-strength winds.

PANDANUS: A shrublike tree from Asia whose strong and supple willowlike leaves are used in the Pacific for weaving fine mats and many household items.

REPAKAK, JIRUKLI: Parts of the rigging for a fixed sail that can be changed to alter the canoe's sailing direction.

TARO: A tropical plant whose long, carrot-shaped root is cooked and eaten as an important source of carbohydrates (starch).

TYPHOON: A hurricane in the Pacific area, having violent winds from 80 to 200 miles per hour.

WOMEN'S PAVILION: A special *fale* or open-sided house (thatched roof, stone or coral floor and wooden pillars) where women gather to work, weave and talk.